DOWNTOWN DINOSAURS

One of the funniest authors for children, Jeanne Willis has been writing since she was five and is the author of many children's books including *Tadpole's Promise*, *Who's in the Loo*, *Bottoms Up* and the hugely popular *Dr Xargle* series.

She has won numerous awards including the Smarties Prize, the Red House Children's Book Award and the Sheffield Children's Book Award.

An enormously popular cartoonist and illustrator, Arthur Robins has illustrated bestselling books by Laurence Anholt, Martin Waddell and Michael Rosen, including *Little Rabbit Foo Foo*, and has even produced some stamps for the Royal Mail.

Available in the
Downtown Dinosaurs series:

Dinosaur Olympics
Dinosaurs in Disguise

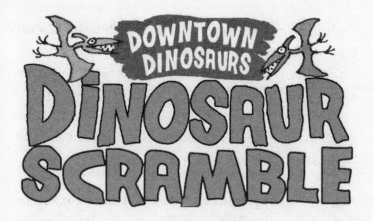

DOWNTOWN DINOSAURS

DINOSAUR SCRAMBLE

JEANNE WILLIS

Illustrated by Arthur Robins

Piccadilly Press • London

For Brenda Gardner, who is no dinosaur.
J. W.

For Alan Dempsey, an interesting old fossil.
A.R.

First published in Great Britain in 2013
by Piccadilly Press Ltd,
5 Castle Road, London NW1 8PR
www.piccadillypress.co.uk

Text copyright © Jeanne Willis, 2013
Illustrations copyright © Arthur Robins, 2013

A catalogue record for this book is available
from the British Library

ISBN: 978 1 84812 315 1

1 3 5 7 9 10 8 6 4 2

Printed and bound by CPI Group (UK) Ltd, Croydon, CR0 4YY
Cover design by Simon Davis
Cover illustration by Arthur Robins

CHAPTER 1

POACHED EGG

There was great excitement at the Stigson household in Fossil Street, Uptown. It was breeding season for the stegosaurs and Mrs Stigson was about to lay an egg. Her only son, Darwin, was longing for a new baby in the family. He'd had a brother once, but while most children would be glad that their little brother had been eaten by a T. Rex, Darwin really missed having someone to play with.

He was great friends with his mad Uncle Loops, but there was a big age gap between them – over one hundred and eighty years. While he was good for musical farts and burping competitions, Uncle Loops was rubbish at football – although his walking frame came in useful for penalty practice.

'It might be a little sister,' said his mother, pacing up and down expectantly.

Darwin didn't care whether it was a boy or a girl, as long as he could put it in goal.

'*I* know what it's going to be,' said Uncle Loops.

Darwin's father gave him a sideways glance. 'Really? You can see into the future?'

Uncle Loops felt around for his glasses and put them on. 'Dang! I can't even see into the present. Fat Phyllis sat on my spectacles!' he said, peering blindly through the shattered lenses. He glared at the mastodon sitting next to him on the sagging sofa.

'That's no way to speak to Mrs Merrick,' said Mrs Stigson. 'She's come to help.'

'Come to help herself to our food, more like,' muttered Uncle Loops.

The egg wasn't due to be delivered until after dinner, but knowing Mrs Stigson had several buns in the oven, the greedy mammoth's timing was perfect.

'I'll take those, Lydia,' Mrs Merrick said, grabbing the loaded baking tray. 'As your midwife, I'd advise you not carry heavy objects in your condition. Think of your little one!'

'Think of your big one!' grumbled Uncle Loops, prodding her bottom with his stick as she hoovered the cherries off the cakes with her trunk.

But Darwin wasn't hungry. All he could think

about was the egg. He decided that while he didn't mind if he had a brother or a sister, it would be good to know beforehand. His mother had asked him to name it and he didn't want to waste time coming up with Brenda and Beyoncé if it turned out to be a Bertie.

'Uncle Loops, do you really know what the baby is going to be?' Darwin asked him.

'Eh?'

Being elderly, Loops was somewhat hard of hearing, so Darwin had to raise his voice. 'DO YOU KNOW WHAT THE BABY IS GOING TO BE?' he shouted.

'Yes, it's going to be . . *noisy*!' said Uncle Loops, turning his hearing aid down.

Mrs Merrick shushed him, spraying the room with crumbs. 'A lady needs peace and quiet when she's on the nest!' she bellowed, poking him with a cake fork. 'Augustus, go and have a nap.'

Uncle Loops tapped his hearing aid. 'Have a what? Oh, is the bathroom free?'

'She said *nap*, Uncle,' said Darwin, 'not cr—'

'I can do both,' interrupted Loops. 'I often nod off on the toilet when I'm having a number two.'

Darwin helped him up.

'You're such a good son,' said his mother.

'Even so,' said Mrs Merrick, marching Darwin to the front door, 'laying eggs is women's business. Now run along and play with the ankylosaur twins.'

'But I want to stay and watch,' said Darwin.

'And *I* want another cake, but I shan't get one,' said Mrs Merrick. 'Off you go!'

Just as Darwin was leaving, Sir Stratford Tempest arrived. He was wearing a silver spacesuit but even with the helmet on, it was impossible to disguise the fact that he was a triceratops.

'I'm absolutely furious!' he said. 'I've just walked off the set of my new film.'

'Which one?' asked Darwin, ducking as Sir Tempest swung his light sword.

'*Star Boars*,' he said. 'My agent promised I'd be Luke Piewalker, but no! The director wants me to play Daft Vadar. It's preposterous!'

He removed his helmet, pulled out a hanky and blew his overly large nose loudly.

'I need to be among friends,' he snivelled, pushing past Darwin. 'Is your papa in?'

'Yes, but Mum's laying an egg. It might be better if you came back tomorrow.'

Sir Tempest dismissed him with a dramatic flourish. 'Tomorrow may never come!' he cried.

'I may be in a galaxy far, far away!'

As much as he would have liked to have been there when the egg was laid, Darwin was glad he was out of the house now that Sir Tempest was inside it, and went off to find his friends. His parents could comfort the neighbourhood drama queen.

'Fix me a drinkypoo,' whined Sir Tempest collapsing on the sofa. 'I'm in agony!'

Mrs Stigson stopped puffing and panting for a second and gave him a withering look. '*You're* in agony? Oh per-*lease*. Try laying an egg that's bigger than your head.'

Sir Tempest grabbed a drink from Mr Stigson and clutched his heart as if he'd been shot.

'What a wicked thing to say. You know I can't have babies.'

'Why's that, Sir Tempest?' flirted Mrs Merrick. 'Are you unlucky in love?'

He leapt up before she could sit on his knee. 'Not as unlucky as you. I've had lots of proposals but having triceratots would ruin my career and yet . . . I would so *love* to hear the clatter of tiny horns.'

He wrung out his hanky and dabbed frantically at the tears before they rusted his costume.

'You're so lucky to be parents,' he sobbed, then suddenly his piggy eyes lit up. 'Ha ha! When the egg hatches, I could be its godfather, couldn't I? Lydia, hurry up and push. I want to see my godchild.'

Mrs Stigson gritted her teeth. 'Please get him out of here, Maurice.'

'Yes, Maurice, take him to the Swine Bar,' said Mrs Merrick, manhandling Mr Stigson out of his own home just as Uncle Loops was coming down on the stairlift.

'Whoa!' cried Uncle Loops, staring at Sir Tempest's costume in disbelief. 'So much tin foil! I've never seen a ready meal that big before.'

'I'm Daft Vadar,' insisted Sir Tempest.

'Welcome to my world,' said Uncle Loops, settling himself back onto the sofa.

Mrs Merrick pushed Sir Tempest into the front garden after Mr Stigson, slammed the door behind them and went to make Mrs Stigson more comfortable. The egg was about to arrive and she was becoming very agitated.

'Phyllis,' said Mrs Stigson, 'I've a horrid feeling someone's watching through the gap in the curtains.'

'You're imagining things,' said Mrs Merrick, drawing them back. She let out a sharp scream and banged on the window.

'Go away, you disgusting, hairy little monster!'

'Is it Boris the Mayor?' groaned Mrs Stigson.

But it wasn't, it was Ozzi the australopithecus and his pet cynognathus, Nogs. Mrs Merrick went over to the drinks cabinet, grabbed the soda siphon, opened the window and squirted them with it.

'And I hope it makes your fur sticky!' she yelled as they skittered off.

'The egg's coming!' yelled Mrs Stigson.

'Egg?' said Uncle Loops. 'I thought we were having beans tonight.'

To everyone's relief, the stegosaur egg arrived quickly. Mrs Merrick checked the shell for cracks, declared that it was perfect and placed it gently in the nest next to Mrs Stigson.

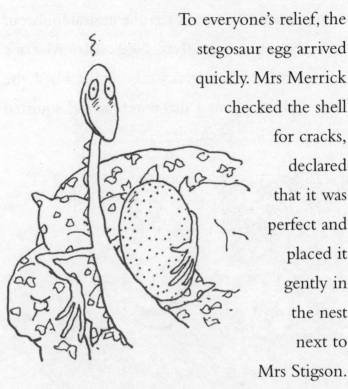

'Congratulations!' she said. 'I expect you'd like a sleep now.'

'Just had one, thanks,' said Uncle Loops.

'What I'd really like is a nice long shower,' said Mrs Stigson. 'Could you help me up the stairs, please? I'm a bit wobbly.'

'Not as wobbly as Phyllis,' said Uncle Loops.

'You hold your tongue and keep an eye on that egg,' said the mastodon.

While his mother and Mrs Merrick were in the bathroom, Darwin came home. He'd had great fun sword-fighting with Frank and Ernest and now he was looking forward to seeing the egg. He could hear Uncle Loops snoring though the open window and smiled, but as he let himself in, his smile rapidly faded.

'Ozzi! What are you doing here?' he gasped.

The australopithecus was standing near the nest with a large shopping bag and there was something in it . . . something egg-shaped! Darwin tried to grab it, but suddenly Nogs shot out from under a table, tripped him up and escaped out of the door with his master.

'Wake up, Uncle!' cried Darwin. 'Ozzi's taken the egg!'

Uncle Loops rubbed his eyes and peered at the nest. 'What's that, then?' he said.

Darwin stared in amazement. It was an egg – there was no mistaking it. So what had Ozzi stolen? He looked round to see if anything similar was missing, but his football was still there and so were all the melons.

'Uncle Loops, Ozzi definitely took something big and round. What could it be?'

'Phyllis?' he said.

Just as he spoke, Mrs Merrick came back downstairs with Mrs Stigson.

'Good egg! Well done, Mum,' said Darwin, as if everything was fine. Given that nothing was missing, he decided not to mention the fact that Ozzi had broken in. It would only upset her and if she knew Uncle Loops had fallen asleep on egg-duty, and he'd be in big trouble.

Mrs Stigson looked at the egg quizzically. 'Phyllis, does my egg look the same to you? I'm sure it was greeny-blue, not bluey-green.'

The mastodon rolled her eyes and patted Mrs Stigson gently. 'All that egg-laying made your eyes water. You're not seeing straight, dear.'

There was a loud knock on the front door, followed by several other loud, impatient knocks.

'All right, I'm coming. No need to break the door down, Maurice!' shouted Mrs Merrick, going to let him in. 'Next time, remember your key.'

But it wasn't Mr Stigson standing on the doorstep. Mrs Merrick's sudden silence worried Mrs Stigson to the tip of her tail.

'Oh no!' wailed Mrs Stigson, going to see what was wrong. 'Please tell me it's not a T. Rex.'

It was worse than that. It was *two* T. Rexes! And one of them was wearing high heels.

'We've got an offer you can't refuse,' said Flint Beastwood.

CHAPTER 2

SCRAMBLED STEG

'You can't come in!' said Mrs Merrick firmly.

Flint Beastwood straightened his hat, ground his cigar out on the doormat and leered at Mrs Merrick in a very sinister way.

'Do you know what "Tyrannosaurus Rex" means?' he said.

'I thought the pub quiz was on Thursdays,' grumbled Uncle Loops.

Despite being frightened of the deadliest carnivore who'd ever ruled Downtown, Darwin was very clever for a stegosaur and was keen to show off his knowledge. He crept out from behind the sofa and put his hand up. 'Ooh . . . I know what Tyrannosaurus Rex means, Mr

Beastwood! It means "Tyrant Lizard King".'

Flint flashed him a horrible, toothy grin. 'It means I can do whatever I like,' he said, pushing past Mrs Merrick and steering the other T. Rex towards the sofa where Uncle Loops was sitting. 'Get up, Granddad,' he said. 'It's bad manners not to give your seat up for a lady.'

Uncle Loops looked the female T. Rex up and

down, folded his arms and refused to move. 'I see no lady,' he said.

Flint Beastwood narrowed his tiny black eyes and thrashed his tail as if he was about to pounce. 'Have you got some kind of beef with my woman?' he growled.

'*Beef?*' exclaimed Uncle Loops. 'Are you nuts? I'm a herbivore.'

Up until then, Mrs Stigson had been trying desperately not to draw attention to herself or her egg but if she didn't apologise on Uncle Loops's behalf, she was afraid the furniture might suffer the consequences. The last time Flint had come round, he'd trashed the place and they'd only just redecorated.

'Sorry about Uncle Loops,' she said. 'He only said he could see no lady because his glasses are broken. He can't see anything much. He's one hundred and ninety, you know.'

'Well, if he wants to be one hundred and ninety-one, he'd better let my fiancée sit down,' said Flint.

'You're getting married?' spluttered Mrs Merrick.

It came as a great surprise to them all – and not a good one. For as long as they'd known him, Flint had been dating a velociraptor called Liz

Vicious. She was as evil as they came, but at least she was a different species, which meant she couldn't have children with Flint. The last thing the herbivores needed was more T. Rexes.

'Yes,' said Flint, putting his scaly arm around his wife-to-be. 'Tara Boomdeeay is indeed the future Mrs Beastwood.'

'Tara *Boomdeeay*?' snorted Mrs Merrick. 'Tara *Boomdeeay*? Like the song?'

'Ta-ra Boomde-eay!' trilled Uncle Loops. 'I do like a sing-along.'

But Tara had heard all the jokes before and couldn't wait to change her name to Beastwood. 'Oh, shut up,' she said. 'I get enough of that from the bouncers at work when I'm waitressing at your club, don't I, Beastie?' She put her head on Flint's shoulder and gazed up at him dreamily.

For a second it looked as if Flint was going soft, but Mrs Stigson dared not let her guard

drop and, covering her egg with a cookery magazine, she tried to stay pleasant and calm.

'A wedding?' she said. 'How romantic. Have you set a date yet, Miss Boomdeeeay?'

'Saturday,' said Flint.

Tara patted her bulging stomach fondly. It was rather large and everyone had assumed it was because she'd just swallowed an Uptowner, but as it turned out, that wasn't the case at all.

'I'm expecting an egg,' she said.

'Just call me Daddy,' said Flint proudly.

Right then, there were plenty of names the neighbours of Fossil Street wanted to call him, but Daddy wasn't one of them. They had hoped that one day Beastwood's reign of terror would end and they'd be free to wander where they pleased without fear of bumping into him and his ruthless gang from Raptor Road. But if he had a child, it would carry on his deadly dynasty until the herbivores were hunted to extinction.

'Congratulations to you both,' said Mrs Stigson through gritted teeth.

'Yes, congratulations,' muttered Mrs Merrick. 'I hate to be rude, but could you leave now? Lydia is rather exhausted. After all, she has just laid —'

'— the table!' interrupted Mrs Stigson,

anxious not to draw attention to her egg.

Uncle Loops heard the words 'table' and 'laid' and thought it was teatime. 'Oh good. I hope there's trifle,' he whooped.

'Trifle?' said Tara. 'Flint, we could have trifle for pudding at our wedding, couldn't we? Only with sausage instead of sponge. You'll do that for us, won't you?' she asked Mrs Stigson.

Mrs Stigson's jaw almost hit the rug. '*Me?*'

The two T. Rexes nodded in a way that suggested a refusal would cause them great offence.

'I want you to do the catering for our Big Day,' said Tara. 'All the food and that. Everyone says you're the best cook around.'

'What my princess wants, she gets,' added Flint. 'We've come to discuss the menu.'

Mrs Stigson went pale. It was true that she ran a very popular catering business but all her clients were herbivores. Planning a wedding feast for carnivores was way beyond her experience.

'I'm flattered to be asked . . .' she said, trying to wriggle out of it politely.

'You'll be flattened if you refuse,' said Flint.

'But I'm no good at cooking meat!' she wailed. The very thought of it made her gag.

Flint and Tara laughed between themselves.

'She can't cook meat. Ha, ha. That's a good one!' hooted Flint.

'We don't want it cooked!' said Tara. 'We want it *raw*! I reckon brontosaurus snouts in bone-

marrow jelly to start, nanosaurus rissoles for mains, then sausage trifle for pudding. What do you think?'

Mrs Stigson thought she was going to be sick. Scared as she was, she just couldn't face the job.

'I'm sure there must be some very nice carnivore caterers Downtown,' she said.

Flint Beastwood thrummed his claws. 'There's no such thing as a *nice* carnivore,' he said, 'and if you refuse us, I will prove just how *nasty* carnivores can be.'

'Here,' said Tara, pointing to Mrs Stigson's

cookery magazine, 'let's have a flick through. You can substitute the revolting veggies in the recipes for meat.'

Mrs Stigson hesitated. If she gave Tara the magazine, her egg would be exposed and if there was one thing she'd hate to see on the menu, it was scrambled steg.

'Bung it over, then,' said Tara. 'We ain't got all day.'

'But the recipes in there are rubbish. Very old-fashioned,' said Mrs Stigson hastily.

'So? I'm prehistoric,' said Tara Boomdeeay. 'I like retro.'

Before anyone could stop her, she darted forward and snatched the magazine.

'Oh my Godzilla!' she said. 'Look, Beastie, it's an egg. I've gone all broody.'

'And I've gone all hungry,' said Flint Beastwood, scooping it up in his hat.

He stalked around the room, taunting Darwin with it. 'How would you like your kid brother or sister – fried or boiled?'

Darwin tried to stand up to him. 'Give it back to Mum!' he shouted. 'You've already eaten my brother, Livingstone! Is there no end to your wickedness?'

Flint Beastwood put his finger to his lips thoughtfully. 'Er . . . No,' he said.

'Excuse me, what are you doing in here, mister?' screeched Sir Tempest, who had just arrived back from the Swine Bar with Mr Stigson. He'd had a shandy and, now filled with courage, he went for Flint with his light sword.

'He's got our egg, Maurice!' wailed Mrs Stigson. 'Do something!'

'I wouldn't if I were you,' said Flint, threatening to tip the egg out of his hat. 'One false move and this baby gets smashed.'

The Stigsons froze.

'Please,' begged Mr Stigson. 'We'll do anything you ask.'

'Yes, you will,' said Flint. 'You can be the waiter at my wedding along with your remaining son and what remains of your uncle. You in the helmet — you can provide the entertainment and be master of ceremonies.'

The sword drooped in Sir Tempest's hand. 'Call my agent by all means but I think you'll find I'm fully booked,' he bleated.

Flint flipped the egg up in the air.

'Okay, okay, I'll do it!' said Sir Tempest, trying to catch the egg. Flint caught it in his hat and, as the triceratops crashed to the floor in a heap, he stood on his helmet.

'Mrs Merrick!' said Beastwood. 'You will be on washing-up duty, and as for the lovely Lydia, well, you know what you have to do if you want your egg back in one piece.'

'The catering,' she sighed as the happy couple left with her egg.

'Don't worry, Mum,' said Darwin. 'I'll get your egg back if it kills me.'

Unfortunately, there was every chance it would.

CHAPTER 3

RISSOLES

'I'll never get these nanosaurus rissoles ready in time for the wedding tomorrow,' sighed Mrs Stigson. She shuddered as she reached into a bowl of mince and tried to roll it into balls. Flint Beastwood had sent a delivery van round with all the ingredients for the feast as no

herbivore in their right mind would risk shopping in carnivore territory. Unfortunately, the meat had come from the market in Raptor Road and as it had been hanging in the sun for several months, it was riddled with maggots and stank.

'I'll open the windows,' said Mr Stigson,

gagging. 'Where's Darwin? I thought he was meant to be helping.'

Mrs Stigson garnished the rissoles with torosaurus toenails and put the tray in the fridge. 'I haven't seen him since breakfast,' she said. 'He told me he was going to No Man's Land to play keepy-uppy with Frank and Ernest. With this terrible smell, I couldn't blame him.'

It wasn't a total lie. Darwin had gone to No Man's Land but it wasn't to play football with the ankylosaur twins. He'd spent a few days planning and now, strictly against his parents' wishes, he'd decided to go and get the stolen egg back from Flint Beastwood. He had to be fast, so he could get back and help his mum, and going through No Man's Land and the Primeval Forest was the quickest route.

It wasn't the *safest* route, though, not by a long stretch – apart from swamps and quicksand there was always the danger of running into a pack of ravenous carnivores. The chances of bumping into a baryonyx were particularly high, especially during the breeding season. They were mostly butchers by trade and young herbivores were a prized delicacy.

Darwin tried to put these thoughts to the back of his mind as he picked his way through the undergrowth.

He usually felt quite confident walking round the edge of the forest because he could still see the playground. It was busy with parents pushing their baby stegosaurs and triceratops on the swings. If something tried to eat him, he could always yell for help. But today he was going across the middle of the forest – through the deepest, darkest part – in order to shave at least an hour off his journey. He was usually very brave, but knowing he was no match for the kind of predators that lurked among the trees, he felt panicky as soon as he left the well-trodden path.

Every time a twig cracked or a small, furry animal squeaked, he almost jumped out of his scaly skin. Rather than run back the way he came, he used an old trick that Uncle Loops had taught him to conquer his fear, which involved marching briskly to a rude rugby song. He smiled as the words came back to him, swung his arms and sang.

'*There once was a brontosaurus,*

His name was Big Bad Billy.

He was brash and brawny, bonkers and bad

But he had a tiny —'

Before he could finish the first verse, something slipped out of the shadows –

something shaped like his worst nightmare. It was a velociraptor, and not just any old velociraptor – it was Flint Beastwood's ex-girlfriend. She blew on her claws and looked at Darwin sideways.

'Keep singing,' she said.

Darwin gulped. The last time he'd seen Liz Vicious she was happy and well-fed but he was shocked to see how thin and mad she looked.

'Finish the song, veggie,' she insisted. 'What did Big Billy have that was so tiny?'

Darwin didn't like to say, so he changed the lyrics. 'Big Bad Billy had a tiny w-woolly hat,' he said. 'To fit his tiny head.'

Liz Vicous pulled a face and circled round him. 'Are you out of your tiny mind?' she said. 'Wandering all alone in the forest when I feel like *killing* somebody?'

'Anyone in p-p-particular?' stammered Darwin. 'Only please can it not be me? Mum has already lost one son and now Flint Beastwood has stolen her egg.'

At the mention of her ex-boyfriend's name, the velociraptor's face went a funny shade of purple and she threw herself on the ground and frothed at the mouth. 'I hate him! I hate him! I hate him!' she cried.

'Dad's not keen on him either,' said Darwin. 'He told me not to go after him but I'm worried Mr Beastwood won't give the egg back after the wedding, even though he promised.'

'Flint's getting married?' wailed Liz Vicious. 'Don't tell me he's marrying that silly little waitress who works at The Prehysterical.'

'OK, I won't,' said Darwin, afraid that she'd rip his head off if he did, but there was no fooling a velociraptor.

'He's marrying Tara Boomdeeay, isn't he?' she roared. 'I'm going to kill him, then I'm going to kill her.'

'Good,' said Darwin. 'Mum will be happy. Can I go now, please?'

He tried to dodge past her, but the velociraptor

pulled him back by his beanie hat. 'Not so fast. I'm coming with you.'

She grabbed his hand and dragged him through the trees at breakneck speed, muttering darkly about how much she'd done for Flint and how much she'd like to bite his nose off and spit it out for proposing to someone else.

'I thought he *loved* me!' she said. 'What has Boomdeeay got that I haven't?'

Darwin thought about it but it was hard to think when he was being bounced over bushes. 'An egg!' he blurted. 'She's expecting Flint's egg.'

Liz Vicious screeched to a halt. For a moment, she looked as if she was about to burst into tears, then her expression changed.

'I'm not going to rip him to shreds,' she said. 'I'll get my revenge another way.'

'How?' wondered Darwin. Liz gave him a gruesome smile.

'I'm going to help you get your mother's egg back,' she said. 'It will kill him. Flint hates being outwitted, especially by herbivores. He'll be a laughing stock, and Boomdeeay won't want to marry him!'

'I don't need your help, thank you,' said Darwin. 'I'll just sneak into The Prehysterical and grab it.'

Liz Vicious rolled her eyes and tickled him under the chin with her foreclaw. 'You're bright for a steggy but you're a whole lot dimmer than a velociraptor. If you just nick the egg, Beastwood will be round your place like a shot to steal it back – you'd be the number one suspect. We've got to be cleverer than that.'

Without giving Darwin a chance to discuss it, she tucked him under her skinny arm and with great leaps and bounds she carried him out of the forest and headed Downtown. Darwin had only been there once before, but the smell was something he'd never forgotten. It came from the meat market and the nearer they got, the worse it became. Darwin was already feeling travel sick and the stench of rotten plesiosaur steaks and dimetrodon chops made his stomach heave.

'Can we stop for a second?' he pleaded. 'I'm going to be sick!'

To his relief, Liz Vicious put him down but as he ran behind the sausage stall to throw up, he almost fell over a cynognathus chewing on a mastodon bone. It was Nogs, which meant that Ozzi would be somewhere close by.

Darwin looked around and there, over by the burger van was the australopithecus. He had something in his wheelbarrow – something large and round, hidden under a blanket of filthy old megalatherium fur. Whatever it was, he was trying to sell it but the baryonyx on the burger stall was driving a very hard bargain.

'A *mammoth* laid it?' said the baryonyx, as Ozzi whisked back the fur to reveal a greeny-blue egg. 'Are you having a laugh? Mammoths are mammals, mate. They don't lay eggs, they give birth. Don't they teach you nothing at school?'

Ozzi stamped his foot and held his hairy hand out.

'It's no good begging,' said the baryonyx. 'Now go home and evolve.'

Ozzi bared his bottom in protest but as the baryonyx blanked him, he decided to try somewhere else. Ozzi went to pull the fur back over the egg to keep it warm – but it had gone!

'Don't look at me, pal,' said the baryonyx. 'I never took it, it was her!'

He was pointing at Liz Vicious who was leaning against his van with a big, round bulge under her blouse. Ozzi spotted it, gnashed his teeth and jumped up and down in a fury.

'What are you going to do about it, little fuzzball?' she said, hitting him round the head with her handbag. 'Come along, Darwin. We need to sneak into The Prehysterical before

Flint gets back. He visits his therapist at two. We have half an hour to do the deed.'

'What deed?' asked Darwin.

'We're going to swap Ozzi's egg for your mum's,' she said. 'Flint won't notice until it hatches. I wish I could see his face when he realises it's not a stegosaurus!'

'I wonder who laid it?' said Darwin. 'It looks like a stegosaurus egg but then most dinosaur eggs look pretty similar.'

'Whatever it is, I hope it bites him when it hatches,' said Liz Vicious as they approached Flint Beastwood's headquarters. Thankfully, there were no bouncers on the door in the day, so it was just a matter of creeping past the barman and up the stairs to Flint's flat.

'I've still got the keys!' said Liz, rattling them triumphantly.

But when he peeked through the letterbox,

Darwin could see Mr Cretaceous and Terry
O'Dactyl. Flint had clearly told the dangerous
deinosuchus and the terrible pterandon to stand
guard over Mrs Stigson's egg.

'How on earth will we get past them?' he
sighed.

Chapter 4

Egg Surprise

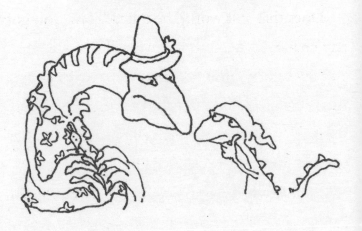

Darwin had to think of a way to get Mr Cretaceous and Terry O'Dactyl out of Flint's flat fast or he'd never get the egg back.

'Maybe we could set the fire alarm off,' he whispered. 'That might distract them.'

'There aren't any,' said Liz. 'Carnivores aren't

big on health and safety.'

Darwin had another think. There was no way he could go home empty-handed. He looked around for inspiration and spotted an old payphone on the wall.

'Does that still work?' he asked. 'Have you got any change? I need to make a call.'

The velociraptor fiddled about in her purse, then hesitated. 'Don't you dare ring the police,' she said. 'I don't want them sniffing around. I'm wanted for crimes against nature.'

But Darwin had no intention of getting the law involved. He'd had a brilliant idea. He would phone up Mr Cretaceous and pretend to be Flint. He was good at doing impressions and even if he couldn't mimic Beastwood exactly, the deinosuchus wasn't the cleverest crocodile in the creek. There was a good chance he'd fall for it.

'What's Flint's number?' he said, picking up

the phone receiver. He heard the call tone and, putting a coin in the slot, he dialled the number Liz had told him.

'Hello?' answered the dangerous deinosuchus. 'Is that you, Mummy?'

Darwin coughed to stop himself laughing and went into Flint mode, complete with crackly noises to help disguise his voice.

'No, it's Mr Beastwood,' he said.

There was a pause.

'Mr Peasgood?' said Mr Cretaceous. 'Speak up, it's a very bad line.'

Darwin tried again with a few less crackles.

'It's Flint,' he growled. 'I'm down in the bar.'

Darwin could hear the deinosuchus talking to Terry O'Dactyl. 'It's the boss. He's got a clown in the car.'

'I'm down in the *bar!*' shouted Darwin. 'I'm having my stag do. I want you and O'Dactyl to join me for drinks in The Prehysterical . . . *now!'*

'On our way, boss!' said Mr Cretaceous. 'Shall I bring the egg?'

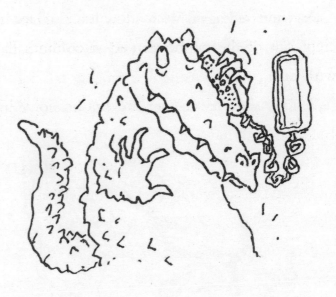

'No, it's underage,' said Darwin. 'Club rules – it must be over eighteen to sit at the bar.'

He put the phone down and hid with Liz Vicious in the stock cupboard as Mr Cretaceous stomped out of the flat and down the stairs with Terry O'Dactyl flapping at his heels.

'I can't wait to see the clown!' screeched the pteranodon. 'But I couldn't eat one. They always leave a funny taste in my mouth.'

As soon as they'd gone downstairs, Darwin crept out of the cupboard and into Flint's flat with Liz.

'I hope they haven't let the egg go cold,' he said, 'or it will never hatch.'

Happily, it was on the radiator, nestled in a furry hat. Darwin gazed at it in wonder. 'Ahh . . . that's my baby brother or sister in there.'

'Yeah, yeah,' said Liz. 'Don't go all gaga on me. I hate soggy veg. Let's swap!'

She reached inside her top and as Darwin lifted the bluey-green egg carefully out of the hat and put it in his beanie, Liz replaced it with the greeny-blue one she'd taken from Ozzi.

'Sorted,' she said. 'I just need to do one more thing before we go.'

She went over to the magnificent portrait of Flint that was hanging on the wall and, using her lipstick, she gave him silly glasses, spots and a ridiculous moustache.

'Right,' she said. 'Let's get out of here. I'll walk you to the end of Raptor Road, then you're on your own.'

'Thank you, Miss Vicious. You've been a good friend to me,' said Darwin as she left him at the edge of the forest. 'Dad says all carnivores are evil and not to be trusted but you've proved him wrong.'

He went to shake her hand but she pulled it away and thumbed her nose.

'I did this for me,' she said. 'Next time, I'll eat you. Get out of here.'

Darwin didn't need telling twice. Hanging on to his hat to stop the egg bouncing, he jogged as fast as he could around the edge of the forest and didn't slow down until he got to the playground in No Man's Land. He sat on a swing to catch his breath and as he swayed gently to and fro, he spoke to the egg.

'This is your brother speaking. It's all right, I'll look after you. I'll soon have you home safe and sound.'

'Talking to yourself?' said a familiar voice. 'Welcome to my world, Damian.'

It was Uncle Loops, lying on the roundabout behind him.

'Everything's spinning!' he wailed. 'Am I having a funny turn?'

Darwin climbed off the swing and helped him. 'No, just a turn on the roundabout,' he said, stopping it.

'That's a relief. I thought it was the park bench,' said Uncle Loops, tottering dizzily. 'I was looking for you, Duncan,' he said. 'I've been here for ages. I was hoping for a game of keepy-uppy with Fred and Ernie, but they never showed.'

'You mean Frank and Ernest?' said Darwin. 'They're not here. I've got a confession to make,

Uncle Loops . . . I went Downtown. I've got something under my hat.'

'That's more than I have,' sighed Uncle Loops.

Darwin took off his beanie and showed Uncle Loops the contents. 'It's Mum's egg! I got it back off Flint Beastwood. Isn't it wonderful? Just think, your baby nephew or niece is inside it.'

'Best place for it,' grumped Uncle Loops. 'It's hell at our house.'

They went back home but as soon as Darwin walked in, he understood why Uncle Loops had walked out. The preparations for Flint's wedding were in chaos. His mother was fretting about the meat trifle, his father couldn't find a clean white shirt to wear and Sir Stratford Tempest was practising his role as master of ceremonies at the top of his voice.

'Laaaaaaaaadies and gentlemen!' he bellowed, banging the dining table with a spoon. 'I give you the bride and groom.'

'Don't use that spoon!' snapped Lydia. 'It's covered in lurdosaurus lard.'

'Well, beg my pardon!' huffed the triceratops, 'but I have to bang something or how will I get the bridesmaids' attention?'

'There's no polite answer to that,' snorted Mrs Merrick. 'Have you sorted out the entertainment yet? How does one amuse a wedding party of thuggish carnivores?'

Sir Tempest reached into his enormous bag and pulled out a jester's hat. 'Ring any bells?' he said, giving it a shake. 'It should do, it has one on each point.'

Mrs Merrick rolled her eyes. 'You'll need more than a funny hat to make a T. Rex laugh,'

she said. 'Have you got a pig's bladder on a stick, Sir Tempest? That's what jesters traditionally carry around with them.'

'No,' he said, 'but I do have a weak bladder. Perhaps you'd like me to put that on a stick? I could hit them over the head with it. I'm sure they'd wet themselves laughing.'

To Darwin's disappointment, no one had even noticed him come in, so he grabbed the lardy

spoon and rapped it on the kitchen door.

'Ladies and gentlemen, I have an announcement to make!' he said.

'You're not getting married are you?' said Uncle Loops. 'I wouldn't recommend it. I've been married fifty times in one hundred and ninety years so I know what I'm talking about, Dennis.'

Darwin took off his beanie hat and showed

his mother the egg. 'No, I've got this back from Beastwood!' he exclaimed.

His mother stopped arranging iguanodon eyeballs on the trifle and cried out loud. 'Darwin, you're my hero! You really are!'

She gave him an air hug, so as not to crack the egg . . . but it was already cracking.

'Quick!' yelled Mrs Merrick. 'It's hatching!'

She cradled the egg in her trunk, placed it in the nest and they all gathered round to watch. They could hear the baby tapping away at the shell from the inside and as the excitement mounted, Sir Tempest started placing bets.

'I bet it's a boy, Maurice. I'll put a fiver on it.'

'A tenner says it's a girl!' Mr Stigson said, smiling and slapping some notes onto the table.

'I bet it's twins!' said Uncle Loops. 'I'm a twin.'

'Oh lordy, there's two of you?' groaned Mrs Merrick.

Mrs Stigson called for hush. The hatchling was about to break through. 'I bet its the sweetest little stegosaurus who ever lived,' she said.

As its head popped out of the shell, the Stigsons took one look at the new arrival and let out a horrified gasp.

'You lost the bet, Lydia,' said Mr Stigson. 'That's no child of ours!'

'It's the funniest-looking stegosaurus I've ever seen,' said Uncle Loops.

There was a very good reason for that.

'It *isn't* a stegosaurus,' said Mrs Merrick.

It was a baby gallimimus!

CHAPTER 5

WHO'S THE DADDY?

Still sticky from hatching, the baby gallimimus gazed up at Mrs Stigson and cheeped.

'It's no good looking at me, little one,' she sighed. 'I'm not your mummy.'

'And *I'm* not your daddy!' said Mr Stigson. 'Explain yourself, Lydia.'

Mrs Stigson folded her arms and harrumphed. 'Don't blame me! I had a funny feeling about that egg all along. The egg I laid was greeny-blue, not bluey-green. I said so at the time, didn't I, Mrs Merrick?'

By now, the gallimimus was swinging off Mrs

Merrick's trunk and she was finding it rather hard to concentrate. 'Did you?' said Mrs Merrick. 'Let me think . . . No . . . Yes, yes, you did. After your shower.'

'Thank you,' said Mrs Stigson. She was angry that Mr Stigson hadn't believed her but it seemed he still wasn't convinced.

'Hmm,' he said. 'Eggs don't just change colour all by themselves.'

'It wasn't all by itself!' said Mrs Stigson. 'Uncle Loops was looking after it.'

All eyes suddenly turned on Uncle Loops.

'You left *him* in charge?' boomed Sir Tempest. 'I wouldn't leave him in charge of a tadpole let alone something as important as a son and heir!'

'We had no choice. You and Maurice weren't here, you were in the Swine Bar,' said Mrs Merrick. 'We only nipped upstairs for a few minutes while we rested. Someone must have come in and swapped the eggs.'

Darwin had a horrible, sinking feeling. He'd guessed what had happened and wanted to tell everybody for his mother's sake, but he didn't want to get Uncle Loops into trouble. Thankfully, he didn't have to. Uncle Loops was perfectly capable of putting his own foot in it without any help from his nephew.

'I didn't see anyone swapping anything,' Uncle Loops said, 'but then, I was asleep at the time.'

Mr Stigson threw his arms in the air and groaned. 'You were asleep . . . Why would you do that?'

'You try staying awake when you're one hundred and ninety!' said Uncle Loops. 'It's harder than it looks.'

Mr and Mrs Stigson looked as if they were about to throttle him. It was no good, Darwin had to say something.

'Please stop picking on Uncle Loops. Ozzi is the one to blame,' he said.

The australopithecus had played more practical jokes on the neighbours of Fossil Street than anyone could count. He loved to meddle

and cause mayhem and when they heard his name, they knew there was every likelihood that he was the culprit.

'I found him in the house when I came back from Frank and Ernest's,' explained Darwin, 'but there was still an egg in the nest, so I thought he'd stolen something else, although I couldn't see what. He must have had your egg in his bag, Mum.'

Mr Stigson slumped down on the sofa. 'Ozzi,' she sighed. 'I might have known.'

'Why didn't you stop him?' said Sir Tempest, putting up his fists. 'I'd have knocked his block off. I've got a marvellous left hook. I was in a boxing film called *The Champ*.'

'It was called *The Chump*,' said Mrs Merrick, 'and you couldn't knock the skin off a rice pudding. I'm sure Darwin tried his best to catch the egg thief.'

'I did,' said Darwin, 'but Nogs tripped me up.'

'Nogs was here?' wailed Mrs Stigson. 'I bet he's left fleas in the rug.'

She scooped up the baby gallimimus protectively and it opened its mouth wide to be fed.

'I don't even know what it eats!' she cried. 'It needs its real mother.'

Mr Stigson took the baby gallimimus from her and gave it to

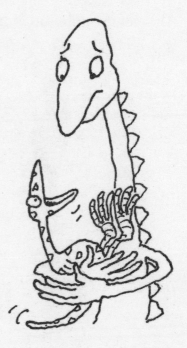

Darwin. 'Your chum Dippy Egg was a gallimimus, wasn't he, son? What did he eat?'

'A bit of everything. He was an omnivore.' Darwin smiled, fondly remembering his friend. Dippy Egg used to be Flint Beastwood's slave and when Darwin was kidnapped by the carnivores and held captive at The Prehysterical, the gentle gallimimus had looked after him. In

return, Darwin taught Dippy how to read and since then, he'd gone abroad to study quantum physics at university.

'I'll mash up some banana,' said Darwin. 'The baby can manage that without teeth.'

'Can I have some? I haven't got any teeth,' said Uncle Loops.

Mrs Stigson watched sadly as Darwin carried the baby to the kitchen. 'I want my egg back, Maurice,' she said.

Mr Stigson sat down next to her and gave her

a comforting squeeze. 'Look on the bright side, Lydia,' he said. 'At least we know where the egg is.'

'Yes, indeedy!' bellowed Sir Tempest. 'How hard can it be to get an egg back from an unintelligent little oik like Ozzi? I think we boys should organise a search party and head down to No Man's Land immediately. I'll go and get my light sword.'

'Good idea, Stratford,' said Mr Stigson. 'He's bound to be there. No Man's Land is australopithecus territory.'

'What if he's cooked it and eaten it already?' wailed Mrs Stigson. 'You know how he likes making fires. Remember the time he set our shed alight?'

It was one of those occasions Mr Stigson preferred to forget.

'Think positive, Lydia!' he said. 'Come on, Sir Tempest. Let's be on our way.'

'We will boldly go!' cried the triceratops theatrically. 'Speaking of which, I'd better go before we set off. May I use your bathroom?'

Darwin had been listening to their conversation from the kitchen. He wanted to butt in and tell them their plan was hopeless but he couldn't get a word in edgeways. Now Sir Tempest was on the loo, he spoke up.

'Dad,' he said.

'Are you coming too, Darwin?' said Mr Stigson. 'Good – the more the merrier.'

'In that case, I'll come,' said Uncle Loops.

'Not that merry,' sighed Mr Stigson. 'Oh, very well, but don't fall for any of Ozzi's tricks, Loops. You know what he's like.'

Darwin held out his hands in dismay. 'There's no point in *any* of us going!' he said. 'Ozzi hasn't got the egg any more.'

His mother looked at him quizzically. 'But you said —'

'I said Ozzi had taken it. I didn't say he still had it.'

'So where is it? Do you know?' asked Mrs Merrick.

Darwin nodded sadly. 'Yes, but it's a very long story.'

However, they all wanted to hear it. So, taking

a deep breath, he told them how he'd bumped into Liz Vicious on the way to Raptor Road and how she'd taken the greeny-blue egg off Ozzi to make a fool of Flint, not realising it was Mrs Stigson's.

'What did she do with it?'

'You're not going to like this,' said Darwin, explaining how he'd sneaked into The Prehysterical and swapped Ozzi's greeny-blue

egg for the bluey-green one in Flint's flat.

His mother looked at him in disbelief. 'You gave Beastwood my egg?'

'I was only trying to help,' he said. 'I thought the egg in Ozzi's wheelbarrow was just some random old one he'd found.'

'I suppose its an easy mistake to make,' said

Mrs Stigson. 'Mrs Merrick didn't even recognise my egg and she delivered it.'

'I was trying to look the other way out of politeness,' said Mrs Merrick. 'But why on earth would Ozzi want to swap your egg for a gallimimus egg?'

'I expect it's a hilarious joke if you're sub-human,' said Mr Stigson. 'Good grief! There he is now at the window, pointing and laughing at us!'

He strode over and banged hard on the glass.

'Be off, you grubby little ape! And take Nogs with you!'

'Finished!' announced Sir Tempest, striding down the stairs. 'Phew, that's better. I should never have had that cauliflower curry. I opened the window but you might want to give it a few minutes before you go in there. Ready to go, men?'

'We're not going,' said Mr Stigson. 'Apparently our egg has fallen into Beastwood's evil clutches. We'll need a far more cunning plan to get it back than I thought. It's no good waving a light sword at him, Stratford, he'll have your hand off.'

'I'll go and ask Lou Gooby what to do,' said Mrs Stigson, turning the oven off. She had a batch of saltopus sausage rolls in there for the wedding and didn't want them to burn.

'There's no need to ask her, dear,' said Mr Stigson. 'I'm perfectly capable of thinking up a far better plan than anything that hippy

mamenchisaurus could come up with.'

'You never have before!' snorted Mrs Merrick. 'I'm coming with you, Lydia. Lou Gooby always knows what to do and, if my watch is right, it's teatime and she always has nice biscuits.'

'Marvellous,' said Sir Tempest, following her out. 'Come along, Maurice. Stop sulking – there might be macaroons.'

Darwin sighed. 'I'll stay here and look after this helpless little creature then, shall I?'

'Hey, I'm not that little!' said Uncle Loops. 'But while you're at it, you can look after the gallimimus too.'

But the gallimimus had other plans.

Chapter 6

Pan-Demonium

Darwin was usually very cool and calm but after an hour with the baby gallimimus, his patience was wearing thin. It was very cute when it was asleep, but it only slept for two minutes after his parents left and now it was wide awake and poking its nose into everything.

It was impossible to keep it amused. Darwin tried reading it a story, but it grabbed hold of the book, tore all the pages out and ate them. He tried rocking it to sleep, but just when he thought it had nodded off, it opened its eyes really wide, clamped its mouth round his nose and started sucking it noisily.

'Maybe it's thirsty,' said Uncle Loops. 'Let's open the whisky.'

Darwin was shocked at the suggestion. 'We can't give a baby whisky!'

'Who said anything about the baby?' said Uncle Loops, helping himself to a glass of Mr Stigson's finest single malt. 'Try singing to it, Dustin. Sing it a lullaby.'

Darwin didn't know any lullabies, so he sang the rugby song Uncle Loops had taught him, but it just seemed to excite the gallimimus even more.

'Maybe you could tell it about the olden days, Uncle Loops,' said Darwin as he tried to stop it chewing the curtains. 'That always puts me to sleep.'

He plonked the baby on his uncle's knee and the ancient stegosaurus told it his life story.

'Long, long ago, during the Ice Age, when I was just a nipper . . .'

'Carry on, Uncle,' yawned Darwin.

He'd heard Uncle Loops's tales of yesteryear a hundred times before and while it had been fascinating the first fifty times, it was just boring now. As Loops recounted the early Jurassic period, Darwin found himself dropping off, just as Uncle Loops cried out in dismay. 'Dang! Now I'm all wet.'

'It's only a baby,' said Darwin, mopping Uncle Loops with a tea towel. 'It's bound to have the odd little accident.'

'It wasn't the baby,' said Uncle Loops.

By now, the baby was fed up with hearing about the time Uncle Loops accidentally married an ichthyosaurus and it ran into the kitchen to play with the saucepans. Darwin chased after it and, remembering how his mother used to give him a wooden spoon to use as a drumstick when he was small, he gave one to the baby. The gallimimus tested it with its mouth, gave a little gurgle of delight, then began to tap the saucepans with it.

'There's a good boy,' said Darwin. 'You play the drums while I go and sit down.'

He settled next to Uncle Loops. 'I've sorted it,' he said, smiling.

But he hadn't at all. After a few moments, the

musical tapping from the kitchen turned into
ear-splitting bangs as the gallimimus smashed the
saucepans harder and harder with the spoon.

'Speak up!' shouted Uncle Loops, but even
yelling, they could still hear nothing but the
clattering of pans.

'*Shut . . . up!*' shouted Darwin.

Suddenly, the baby went quiet and Darwin
felt bad. That was no way to talk to a little one.

He could hear it making muffled squeaks and went to comfort it. To his horror, Darwin saw it had got its head jammed in the milk pan.

Darwin tried to pull it off, but it was stuck tight.

'That happened to me once,' admitted Uncle Loops. 'You'll have to cut its ears off.'

'It hasn't got any ears,' said Darwin. 'I'll try greasing it with butter.'

He found a tub in the cupboard and, taking a handful in his fingers, he rubbed it round the baby's head and the saucepan rim and tried to ease it off.

'Its body warmth should melt the butter soon,' he explained.

'What if it's cold-blooded?' said Uncle Loops.

'I dunno,' panicked Darwin, 'I'll run a hair-dryer over it. Can I borrow yours?'

Uncle Loops lifted up his hat. He was as bald as ping-pong ball. 'Why would I have a hairdryer? Never mind that – you grab its feet, I'll grab the saucepan and we'll pull on the count of three. One, two . . .'

'Three!'

Suddenly, the saucepan came off and Uncle

Loops went reeling out of the open kitchen door and fell down the back steps.

'Are you all right, Uncle?' called Darwin.

'I'm a bit buttered,' he said, 'but I'm not half as buckled as this pan.'

Keeping hold of the gallimimus with one hand, Darwin went to help his uncle up.

'Let's take the baby to the swings and slides,' he said. 'Maybe that'll wear it out.'

No Man's Land was too far for a baby to walk there and home again. Darwin didn't fancy

giving it a piggyback ride if it got tired, so they used his mother's shopping trolley as a pram. It seemed to like it in there and, for the first time that day, it went quiet, fascinated by the trees and clouds. When they got to the playground, it was even happier. It loved the baby swings and it wasn't the only one.

'Wheeeee!' whooped Uncle Loops.

'Aren't you a bit old to be doing that?' said Darwin.

'Ah, don't be a killjoy and give me another push,' said Uncle Loops.

After the swings, the little gallimimus had a turn on the roundabout, which it liked even more. The only trouble was that every time Darwin stopped spinning it, it screeched and everyone kept giving him dirty looks. Finally, he caught the baby mid-spin and carried it kicking and screaming to the sandpit.

'Play in there,' he said, showing it how to build a sandcastle. 'Don't move. I'm just going to make sure Uncle Loops doesn't land in the mud.'

It was too late. He'd warned Uncle Loops not to sit on the end of the slide but he hadn't listened and a very chubby triceratops toddler went whooshing down and booted him right up the backside and into a puddle.

'I don't know what hit me,' said Uncle Loops.

Darwin was very close to hitting him by then. It was hard to know which was worse – trying to look after his elderly uncle or the infant gallimimus.

'Where's the baby?' said Uncle Loops.

'Playing in the sand,' said Darwin.

But it wasn't. When they looked, it was nowhere to be seen. It wasn't in the den under the climbing frame or on the monkey bars or at the top of the slide. It had vanished.

'It must have gone into the Primeval Forest,' gasped Darwin. 'Run, Uncle!'

'I *am* running,' said Uncle Loops, plodding along with his zimmer frame.

Darwin was praying that if they got there quickly, they'd be able to find the baby before a baryonyx did. The little gallimimus might have been a nuisance, but Darwin was attached to it now and he'd hate it to come to any harm.

There was no sign of the gallimimus anywhere near the edge of the forest, so they had

no choice but to look for it in the deepest, darkest part.

'Sing the rugby song, Desmond!' said Loops. 'This place gives me the willies.'

'*There once was a brontosaurus, his name was Big Bad Billy*,' sang Darwin.

The song helped with their nerves but despite searching high and low they still hadn't found the baby, so they sang it over again to keep their spirits up.

'*He was big and he was bad*,' sang Uncle Loops, '*but he had a tiny* — What the hey?'

He stopped singing and pointed towards a cave. He put his head in his hands.

'What is it, Uncle?' whispered Darwin. 'Is it a T. Rex?'

Uncle Loops shook his head and bit his nails.

'Is it a baryonyx?'

Again, Uncle Loops shook his head.

'What can you see? Is it the baby?'

Uncle Loops couldn't see anything now. He'd closed his eyes because he couldn't bear to look.

CHAPTER 7

A GAME OF CHICKEN

Darwin peered into the distance and his heart sank. A chick-sized creature with a beak and long legs was hanging upside down from a hook at the cave entrance. It was the same way the butchers in Raptor Road hung up their meat in the market. Darwin sat down in the grass and sighed.

'Oh no! The carnivores must have got him.'

'Bum!' said Loops. 'Finally I meet someone my own mental age and this happens!

'We can't leave him like that,' said Darwin sadly. 'I'll go and unhook him. We'll give him a decent burial in the back garden.'

'Great,' said Uncle Loops. 'I love a good funeral. I can't wait for my own.'

He was very upbeat about it, but Darwin didn't think it was the right attitude.

'It's all right for you,' he said, 'you've had a long life, but that baby was just out of his egg. He didn't have a very good innings.'

'No, but he had a very good outing. What with the saucepan banging and the swings and slides, he packed more into his short time on earth than most. It's quality of life, not quantity, Desmond,' said Uncle Loops. 'You'll learn that when you get to my age.'

'I'm not Desmond, I'm *Darwin*,' said his nephew.

Uncle Loops rolled his eyes and tutted. 'Stop changing your name, Donald. It's so confusing.'

Darwin let it go. He had bigger things to worry about.

'Pass me the blanket out of the trolley, please,' he said. 'I'll use it to wrap the body.'

He felt tearful as he walked towards the cave

but as he approached, he heard something scuttling about inside. Darwin legged it back and hid in the grass.

'Keep quiet, there's somebody in there!' he hissed at his uncle.

'Eh?' shouted Uncle Loops.

'Shhh! I bet it's the carnivore who killed the baby,' fretted Darwin. 'It's probably coming back to eat it – and us if we're not careful.'

But it wasn't a T. Rex or a baryonyx or even a sabre-toothed tiger.

'Ozzi!' groaned Darwin.

He watched as the australopithecus took the creature down from the hook and squeezed its tummy. It gave a comical squeak — but it wasn't the kind of squeak a baby gallimimus made.

'It sounds like a rubber chicken,' said Uncle Loops.

That's because it *was* a rubber chicken, and when Ozzi squeaked it again, Nogs came running out of the cave, keen to play a game of fetch with it. Once, twice, three times Ozzi

hurled the toy over-arm in their direction for Nogs to chase, and each time, the cynognathus retrieved it like an oversized puppy and dropped it at his master's hairy feet.

'I hope Nogs doesn't smell us,' said Darwin.

'I can smell him from here,' muttered Loops.

They lay low until Nogs got bored with fetching the toy and followed Ozzi into the forest for his afternoon walk.

'It's more of a lurch than a walk really, isn't it?' said Darwin, dusting himself down as Ozzi disappeared among the trees.

'He's only been on two legs for a few hundred years,' said Uncle Loops. 'Give the guy a break.'

They were so happy to think that the gallimimus might still be alive that they were willing to be nice about the australopithecus for once.

'It was just a rubber toy,' chortled Darwin.

'Had me fooled,' said Uncle Loops. 'Shame about the funeral, though. I was looking forward to that. I don't suppose there will be one now.'

Suddenly Darwin froze. He could hear footsteps running through the undergrowth.

'There might be a double funeral yet – yours and mine! Hide, Uncle!'

'First "fetch", now "hide and seek". This is all a big game to you, isn't it, Dawson?' said Uncle Loops.

'No, someone's coming!' whispered Darwin. 'It can't be Ozzi – the footsteps aren't sub-human. It sounds like hundreds of footsteps. Please don't let it be a pack of carnivores!'

He held his breath. The footsteps were getting closer and closer and louder and louder and as he put his hands over his head to protect

himself, a herd of gallimimus thundered over him, landed and ran towards the cave. He watched in amazement as the last gallimimus sauntered along casually at the rear, carrying a baby with a buttery face.

'Dippy, is that you?' exclaimed Darwin.

The gangly gallimimus turned round. Seeing his long-lost friend, his eyes lit up and his mouth stretched into a huge grin.

'Darwin! Hey, how are you doing? And Uncle Loops! You don't look a day over a hundred and eighty. Wow! It's good to see you both.'

Darwin was thrilled to see him too. 'I thought you were at uni,' he said. 'Did you finish your degree?'

'Nah. Quantum physics just wasn't my thing,' said Dippy. 'It was too easy.'

Darwin was amazed. 'So you dropped out?'

Dippy Egg shrugged. 'Yeah, cooking's always been my first love,' he said. 'It's what comes of being half-starved

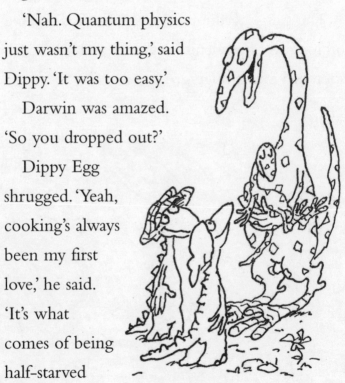

when I was Beastwood's slave. I'm at catering college with those guys.'

He pointed to the flock of teenage gallimimi who had gone in the cave. 'We've been living

there since half-term,' he said. 'We all take turns to cook – mostly vegetarian although sometimes we use insects. Freud Egg over there does a lovely grasshopper in batter.'

Dippy's friend, Freud turned round and nodded modestly. 'You have to get the oil really hot,' he said. 'It needs to be smoking. That's the secret if you want them nice and crispy.'

'Cool,' said Darwin.

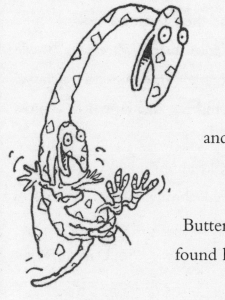

Hearing his voice, the baby gallimimus opened its eyes and held its arms out for a cuddle. 'Meet little Butternut,' said Dippy. 'I found him wandering by the swamp.'

'We've already met,' said Darwin, laughing.

The gallimimus looked at the baby quizzically. 'You're kidding me – how?' He waved Darwin and Uncle Loops inside. 'Come in and tell me all about it. I'll whip you up a cheese soufflé.'

It was very homely in the cave, if a bit cramped but the gallimimi were all very friendly and were falling over themselves to get the stegosaurs to sample their latest recipes.

'Have a piece of lotus loaf,' said one. 'It's made from inner petals steamed in dew with a delicate drizzle of wild orchid jus and served in a moss bun.'

'Lovely – got any ketchup?' asked Uncle Loops.

Dippy Egg rattled about among the shelves and fetched some ingredients.

'So, Darwin, what are you doing in this neck of the woods?' he asked as he dried his hands on a clean apron and grated some woolly mammoth cheese into a dish. 'It's hard to know where to begin,' said Darwin.

'At the end,' said Uncle Loops. 'I've heard it already.'

But Dippy wanted to know everything and by the time the soufflé had risen, Darwin had explained all about Ozzi and the egg swap, and how it had all gone horribly wrong when Liz Vicious got involved.

'Damian brought the wrong egg home,' said Uncle Loops, 'and left me holding the baby.'

'That's not entirely true, is it?' said Darwin, trying to defend himself, but Uncle Loops had to say his piece.

'*Then* he mistook it for a rubber toy, Dopey!' added Uncle Loops.

The gallimimus corrected him gently. 'I'm Dippy.'

'Not as dippy as Dawson,' said Uncle Loops. 'I think he's lost the plot.'

It was no good trying to argue with Uncle Loops, so Dippy gave him some of his soufflé,

which silenced him nicely for a few moments.

'I might have known Beastwood was behind it all,' said Dippy Egg.

Whenever he'd spoken about his old boss in the past, the mere mention of his name would set off his left eye into nervous, winking spasms.

No wonder – he had suffered for years as Flint's slave and if Darwin hadn't helped him escape abroad, goodness knows if he'd still be around to tell the tale.

'I owe you my life, Darwin,' said Dippy, 'and I'm going to do everything I can to help you get your mother's egg back.'

'Make sure it's the right one this time, Dustin,' said Uncle Loops. 'Lydia's egg was pinky-yellow not yellowy-pink.'

'It was greeny-blue!' insisted Darwin.

'Are you colour blind?' said Loops. 'I'd better come with you, Daffy.'

CHAPTER 8

HEY NONNY NO

Meanwhile, Mr and Mrs Stigson and the neighbours had arrived at Lou Gooby's to find her meditating on her nest. Being the largest herbivore on the planet, her eggs were huge.

'Ouch, that must have hurt,' winced Mrs Stigson. 'Are you alright, Lou?'

'Egg-laying most natural thing in world for dinosaur,' she said in her exotic accent. 'Secret is relax.'

'Relax?' snorted Mrs Merrick. 'You try relaxing when you've been the victim of an egg-swapping prank.'

Lou Gooby came out of her yoga pose and looked closely at the mastodon. 'You have laid egg, Mrs Phyllis? How so? You are mammal with hair and udders!'

'Yes, yes,' tutted Mrs Merrick, 'I was talking about Mrs Stigson. Ozzi took her egg and now Flint Beastwood has got it.'

Lou Gooby pressed her claws together and frowned deeply. 'So! Most precious stegosaur egg fall into evil clutch of meat-eating tyrannosaur!'

Mrs Stigson was hoping the mamenchisaurus would tell her not to worry and that all would be well, but she said nothing of the sort.

'Beastwood is mean and cruel egg-eating gangster!' she continued.

By now, Mrs Stigson had come over all emotional. 'What are we going to do, Maurice?' she wailed. 'I loved that egg.'

Like most stegosaurs, Mr Stigson wasn't sure

what to say when his wife was upset, and when he tried, he only made matters worse.

'Beastwood said he'd give it back after his wedding,' said Mr Stigson. 'I'm sure he will, Lydia. He's in love – he must have a heart. He can't be all bad.'

Mrs Merrick rounded on him immediately. 'In *love?*' she snorted. 'Beastwood only loves himself. Honestly, Maurice, if you seriously think he can be trusted, you're wetter than a whale's Y-fronts.'

Lou Gooby got off her nest and stood on her head.

'Now what's she doing?' grunted Sir Tempest. 'This is no time to go bottom up.'

'Shush, it helps her to think. Stop interrupting!' snapped Mrs Merrick as she bent

down and peered through her back legs to catch the mamenchisaurus's eye.

'Are you thinking about serving tea and buns any time soon, Mrs Gooby?' she asked.

Lou blinked slowly and wobbled a little. 'I am thinking of clever way to save most precious egg!' she said.

Mrs Merrick could barely hide her disappointment. 'Can't you do both? How hard can it be to arrange a few cakes on a doily?'

The mamenchisaurus lowered her back legs onto the grass and stood up straight. 'We must fight fire with fire!' she said.

'Is there a fire?' said Sir Tempest, sniffing the air for smoke. 'I do hope the sponge cake hasn't gone up in flames or we'll never hear the end of it, will we, Phyllis?'

'Anyone would think I was obsessed with cakes, the way you go on,' said Mrs Merrick.

'You'd be the first to complain if the macaroons were overdone, Sir Tempest.'

Lou waited for them to stop bickering and explained. 'When I say fight fire with fire, I mean we must beat Beastwood at his own game.'

'But how?' asked Mr Stigson. 'We never beat him at anything, not even tiddlywinks. He cheats and if he still doesn't win, he makes death threats instead. That's hardly fair.'

Lou Gooby tapped her giant snout knowingly. 'We must also do cunning egg swap!' she said.

Fumbling around in her nest, she produced a white egg, which was much smaller than the rest and held it up for them to see.

'This my one bad egg,' she said. 'It will never hatch – take! Paint greeny-blue to make like egg of stegosaur. On wedding day, creep into flat of Flint and swap mouldy mamenchisaurus

egg for egg of Mrs
Stigson!'

'I suppose it's a plan,'
said Mr Stigson, wishing
he'd thought of it.

'It's a great plan!' said
Mrs Stigson, glad that she
hadn't left it down to him.
'Thank you, Lou!'

The mamenchisaurus bowed deeply and
handed her the duff egg. 'Take great care not to
drop or will make most suffocating pong.'

The Stigsons and the neighbours hurried
home. They had just got the key in the door
when Mrs Merrick clutched her trunk and
screwed up her face.

'Have you dropped that egg, Maurice?' she
said. 'Something stinks!'

'Excuse me,' said Sir Tempest, wafting his tail.

'I'm rather windy. It was that vegetable curry.'

Mrs Stigson decided she'd had quite enough of the neighbours for one day and encouraged them to go home. 'Thank you for your support,' she said. 'I need a rest now, if you don't mind. We'll see you at the wedding tomorrow. Goodbye.'

'You haven't got a fruit loaf in the oven? No fairy cakes in the fridge?' wondered Mrs Merrick.

'Just gristly, meaty things,' said Mrs Stigson.

'Goodbye!' said Mrs Merrick.

Mrs Stigson closed the front door behind her and sighed with relief.

'They mean well,' she said, 'but they really get on my nerves . . . Now, where's the baby?' She looked around to see a long, lanky gallimimus sitting on the sofa squished between Darwin and Uncle Loops. She did a double-take. 'No! It can't possibly have grown that quickly.'

'That's Dopey,' said Uncle Loops.

'It's Dippy, Mum.' Darwin grinned. 'He's quit uni. Quantum physics wasn't his thing. He's living with some other catering students. It's OK, one of his friends is minding the chick.'

Mrs Stigson held out her arms and smiled.

'How wonderful to see you, Dippy!'

The gangly gallimimus got up and gave her a hug. 'You too, Mrs S! You're glowing. Hey, Mr Stigson. Who's egg have you got there?'

'Oh, this is a dud,' he said airily as his wife explained about Lou Gooby's cunning egg-swap plot. Darwin thought it sounded great in theory, but he was worried that it might not work in practice.

'How are we going to swap the egg without one of the carnivores spotting us?' he asked.

His parents looked at him blankly.

'I knew there had to be a flaw in Gooby's plan, Lydia,' said Mr Stigson. 'Even if Flint doesn't see us, Mr Cretaceous and Terry

O'Dactyl are bound to be on the look-out. One false move and we'll end up on the meat platter at the wedding.'

Darwin thought about it, and the more he thought about it, the more Sir Tempest's jester costume sprang to mind. It was too big for him to wear and he had the wrong shape head for the cap with bells on, but it would fit a grown gallimimus perfectly. If Dippy went to the wedding in it, Sir Tempest could pass him off as part of the entertainment.

Once inside, he knew his way around the building and could easily slip into Flint's flat without raising suspicion, do the swap and put Mrs Stigson's egg under his jester's cap.

'How do you fancy playing the joker, Dippy?' asked Darwin.

'I'll do anything for a laugh,' said his friend.

Darwin explained, and it was all agreed. So, as Mr Stigson painted Lou's egg a greeny-blue, Darwin went round to Sir Tempest's bungalow to borrow the jester costume. After Dippy had tried it on and Mrs Stigson had taken it in at the waist, she put it to one side and he helped her finish cooking the wedding feast.

'I'm at catering college,' Dippy told her.

'It shows,' said Mrs Stigson, smiling as he made a rose out of a plesiosaur kidney and used it to garnish the tray of sausages.

It was almost midnight by the time they'd finished. All they had to do now was put cling film over the food trays to keep the flies off.

'Why are you bothering?' said Mr Stigson. 'Carnivores like flies on their meat.'

'Dippy insisted,' said Mrs Stigson. 'He has a certificate in food hygiene.'

Just then, Darwin burst out laughing in the front room and they went to see what was so funny.

'It's Uncle Loops!' hooted Darwin. 'Look what he's wearing!'

He'd got the jester costume on. It was far too big for him and the cap had fallen over his eyes, so he couldn't see.

'You wait till you're old and blind!' he wailed.
'Did these pyjamas stretch in the wash, Lydia?'

'There's no fool like an old fool,' said Mr
Stigson.

With surprising speed, Uncle Loops leapt up
and bopped him on the head with a pig's bladder
on a stick that Mrs Stigson had made from left-
over offal.

'Hey nonny . . . *No!*'
yelled Mr Stigson.

'Now who's
laughing?' said
Uncle
Loops
with a
grin.

CHAPTER 9

LONG LIVE THE CARNIVORES

Beastwood's wedding day had arrived and while the carnivorous couple was getting married in the Meating Room in the grounds of The Prehysterical, Mrs Stigson was in Flint's kitchen readying the rissoles for the reception.

'Have you seen the state of this sink?' groaned

Mrs Merrick. 'It's full of blood! It looks like a crime scene. How am I supposed to do the washing up in this?'

'Just put some rubber gloves on and try not to breathe,' said Mrs Stigson, batting away a swarm of bluebottles. 'Maurice, have you finished laying the tables?'

Mr Stigson and Darwin had spent the best part of the morning putting out the cutlery and folding napkins into amusing shapes but, to their

despair, Uncle Loops had kept playing with the spoons and switching the place names but at least now had gone to sleep under a tablecloth.

'Uncle Loops, get up!' said Darwin, whisking the cloth away.

'It can't be morning already,' he said, yawning. 'I've only just gone to bed.'

He wasn't going to get a lie-in, though – Sir Tempest was testing the microphone and had switched the volume up so loud no one could hear themselves think.

'If I wasn't deaf already, I would be now!' complained Uncle Loops.

'Sorry, what?' bellowed Sir Tempest. 'As master of ceremonies, I need to check the sound system to make sure everyone can hear me at the back of the room.'

'They can hear you at the back of beyond!' shouted Mr Stigson, covering his earholes. 'Turn it down, Stratford, you're making the windows vibrate.'

'Testing . . . testing . . .' said the triceratops at the top of his voice. 'One-two, one-two . . . Me-me-me . . . Meee-me-me-meeeee.'

'It's all about you, isn't it?!' yelled Mrs Merrick, charging out of the kitchen and chasing him with a tea towel. She was just about to whop him with it when she caught sight of the wedding cake. It was the size of a small tower block.

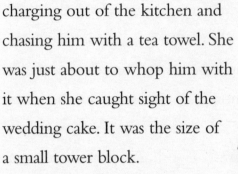

'Oh happy day, it's got *ten* tiers!' she exclaimed as her trunk began to water. 'I could have a whole one to myself and nobody would notice. I'll just go and sniff the marzipan.'

She tiptoed over to the cake and had just stuck her tongue out to taste it when she disturbed something crawling about under the cake stand. It nipped her on the ankle and she let out a piercing shriek.

'What is it?' said Mrs Stigson nervously, hurrying into the hall in her apron to see what all the fuss was about. 'Is it a rat?'

But it was worse than a rat – it was the australopithecus! He had icing sugar in his shaggy eyebrows and was clearly up to no good. Mrs Merrick grabbed a broom and chased him out.

'No nipping, Ozzi! Off you go – and take Nogs with you!'

She'd just got rid of him when Flint Beastwood and Tara Boomdeeay came marching up the path with Mr Cretaceous, Terry O'Dactyl and an assortment of rough-looking relatives and friends.

'Quick, they're coming!' she muttered. 'Everybody get to your posts! Maurice, your zip's undone. Uncle Loops, if you must pick your nose, use a hanky.'

'I used a breadstick,' he said, 'but it's all right, I put it back in the basket.'

Sir Tempest cleared his throat and grabbed the

mic. 'Ladies and gentlemen,' he boomed. 'I give you the bride and groom!'

'You can keep 'em!' heckled Uncle Loops.

Mr Stigson ushered him into the kitchen before he could upset anyone and left him with Dippy, who was waiting patiently for the right moment in the jester's costume.

As soon as the guests were seated, Darwin and his father brought in the banquet, trying not to gag at the great, greasy slabs of flesh they had to serve up. It wasn't a pleasant job and if the herbivores thought Flint Beastwood's table manners were poor, he was an absolute gentleman compared to Tara's father.

Not only did Mr Boomdeeay eat noisily and with his mouth open, he started a rissole fight with the next table which rapidly spread across the entire room until they'd run out of ammunition. Apart from being an awful waste of food, Mr

Stigson was pelted with meatballs, which spattered his best white shirt with mince and gravy.

The bride's mother was no better. Having drunk a large bucket of sherry, she climbed onto the table and, showing off her elderly undies, she danced until she slipped on a custard slick and

landed face down in the trifle.

Seeing that the wedding feast was fast turning into chaos, Sir Tempest tried to calm things down. 'Pray silence for the groom's speech!' he roared.

'You can shut up an' all, you three-horned pachyderm!' cackled Mrs Boomdeeay.

'Don't make me laugh, Mum,' hooted Tara. 'My egg will pop out! Hurry up and make your speech, Beastie, then we can cut the cake. I'm eating for two, remember.'

Flint scraped his chair back and stood up.

'Speech!' screeched Terry O'Dactyl. 'Speech! Speech! Speech!'

'Somebody put a cloth over him!' yelled Mrs Boomdeeay as she picked the jelly out of her ears. 'Speak up, Flint. I'm a trifle deaf.'

The groom waited until Mr Cretaceous had silenced the pteranadon by ramming a napkin ring over his beak, then he began.

'First of all,' he said, 'I'd like to thank all my friends and relatives for coming, especially those of you who escaped from prison just to be here.'

'Prison?' whispered Mrs Stigson who was listening through a gap in the kitchen door. 'I wonder what they were in for?'

'Murderers, the lot of them,' hissed Mrs Merrick. 'And thieves! I just saw Mrs Boomdeeay putting a silver pudding spoon and a salt and pepper set in her handbag. She's stealing from her own son-in-law right under his nose.'

Dippy adjusted his jester suit, checked himself in the mirror and made sure Lou Gooby's egg was safely hidden under his cap and bells.

'Is now a good time to sneak out and do the swap, Mrs Stigson?' he asked.

'Give it a moment,' she said. 'Wait until Flint proposes the toast. They'll all be so busy chinking their glasses, they won't notice you.'

She hovered at the door and listened as Flint continued his speech.

'I would now like to thank my beautiful bride,' he said.

'Not only did she agree to marry me, she is expecting my egg – the first of many, we hope – and my sons and daughters and their sons and daughters will reign supreme over the herbivores forever!'

There was a roar of approval from the guests.

'Smashing!' said Mr Cretaceous, thumping the table with his fist.

Beastwood exchanged an evil smile with the

burly deinosuchus. 'I'll tell you all what *will* be smashing,' he said. 'The stegosaurus egg that I took from the Stigsons. I said I'd give it back, but I think I'll break my promise, and why is that, my friends?'

'Because you're a *carnivore!*' they yelled.

'Did you hear that, Phyllis?' squeaked Mrs Stigson. 'I don't care what Maurice says, I knew we couldn't trust Flint.'

'Dippy,' said Mrs Merrick. 'It's time to make your move. Good luck!'

Flint raised his glass triumphantly. 'I should like to propose a toast. Down with Uptown! Long live the carnivores!'

'Long live the carnivores!' echoed the guests as Dippy made his way quietly across the back of the hall towards the exit, trying not to let the bells on his cap jangle. He was just about to make it through the door when Flint Beastwood spotted him.

'Oh look,' he said. 'The clown's arrived. Come here and make me laugh until my eyes bleed.'

Dippy froze in his tracks. This wasn't part of the plan and he wasn't sure what to do. If he broke into a run it would look suspicious but as he had no jokes up his sleeve apart from the pig's bladder, he worried that Flint might not be amused and attack him. Seeing his dilemma, Sir Tempest tried to come to the rescue.

'The jester will be with you shortly, Mr Beastwood,' he said, 'but first, you must cut the wedding cake – would you and your lovely wife like to step this way?'

He was in two minds about handing them the cake knife – a pair of T. Rexes were dangerous enough and to arm them with a sharp object was seriously asking for trouble. He had a feeling something shocking was about to happen, and he was right. Just as Flint and Tara were about to plunge the blade into the top tier, there was an explosion of crumbs and currants. To the bride and groom's shock, Ozzi burst out of the cake, covered in icing.

'Ta-da!' he whooped, grinning from ear to ear.

His smile soon faded. United in their hatred
of the australopithecus, the guests joined Flint in

a ghastly game of chase. As they cornered Ozzi behind the grand piano, nobody noticed the jester slip out of the room, aided by a small stegosaurus in a waiter's outfit.

'I'll keep a look-out,' said Darwin. 'Good luck, Dippy!'

Chapter 10

Egg on the Face

Having been forced to live at The Prehysterical
since he was an orphan, Dippy knew the place
like the back of his hand. He knew where the
spare key was kept in the basement and had no
trouble remembering the way to Flint's flat on
the top floor. However, once he was inside, he

had great trouble trying to find Mrs Stigson's egg. Darwin had told him it would be inside a hat near the radiator, but it wasn't there.

He had a look in the wardrobe, but apart from Flint's suits and a frilly dress that secretly belonged to Mr Cretaceous, there was no sign of it. He looked under the bed. Maybe Flint had put it in the potty he used when he couldn't be bothered to walk three metres to his bathroom. Dippy knew about the potty because, when he was Flint's slave, it was his job to empty it every day. Unfortunately, Beastwood's latest slave must have died – the potty was full to the brim, and there was no egg.

The egg wasn't under a pillow or in the safe. With a deep sigh, Dippy went over to the fridge – maybe Tara had already boiled it, mashed it with mayonnaise and made it into egg sandwiches. He opened the door and retched. There was a bowl of guts on the middle shelf that had long since past their eat-by date, and a bag of mouldy toes in the salad drawer, but thankfully there was nothing in the egg rack except a row of eyeballs. They were staring at him, so Dippy slammed the door shut and continued his search.

He checked the laundry basket. Seeing that it was empty, he guessed that Tara must have done the washing recently which reminded him to look in the airing cupboard. The boiler was in

there and it was the perfect place to keep an egg nice and warm. He riffled through a stack of towels on the wooden shelf and underneath, wrapped in a pair of Flint Beastwood's lucky pants, was Mrs Stigson's egg.

Dippy lifted it out, pleased to see it was in perfect condition, and put it gently under his cap. Taking great care not to drop Lou Gooby's

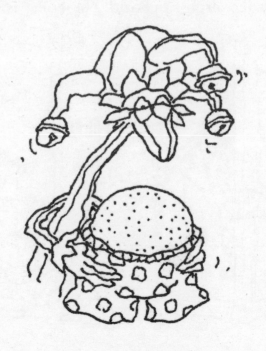

rotten egg, he tucked that inside Flint's Y-fronts and put them back in the airing cupboard. The switch was complete.

Dippy was just congratulating himself on the job when he heard little footsteps charging up the stairs and Darwin came bursting into the flat. He was out of breath and looked extremely worried.

'Terry O'Dactyl saw you leave! He followed you and told Flint and now they're all heading this way!'

'Come on,' said Dippy, 'there's a fire escape on the landing – it's never locked. They won't see us if we go out the back way.'

But it was too late.

'Who won't see you?' growled a familiar voice.

Flint Beastwood had come in the front way. He was standing in his top hat and tails blocking

the doorway with Mr Cretaceous, Terry O'Dactyl and Tara.

'I was just . . . um . . . showing the jester where the toilet was,' said Darwin.

'Do you hear that, Mr Cretaceous?' Flint mocked. 'Young Darwin reckons he broke into my flat so that the clown could use my facilities. Do we believe him?'

'No, boss!' said the deinosuchus, thumping his fist into his palm. 'Want me to flush him down the lavvy?'

Flint shook his head. 'No, no. Flushing is far too good for him, Mr C. He was about to commit a most terrible crime, weren't you, you thieving little sprout?'

Darwin pressed himself against the wall and denied everything. 'No! I'm a herbivore, Mr Beastwood. We never steal.'

The tyrannosaurus threw back his head,

clutched his sides and guffawed, only to be copied by the mad pteranodon who laughed so hard he became hysterical. Flint's face straightened and he slapped him on the beak.

'It's not funny, Mr O'Dactyl,' he hissed,

pointing at Dippy. 'I'm afraid that clown has been fiddling around in my pants and stolen the stegosaurus egg.'

Flint was deadly serious but hearing the word

'pants' tickled Terry O'Dactyl so much, he let out a terrible titter and collapsed in a giggling heap until Mr Cretaceous was instructed to lock him in the wardrobe.

'Have a look in the airing cupboard, Beastie,' said Tara. 'If the clown has nicked it, you can hold him down and I'll rip his head off. That's what marriage is about, innit, babe?'

'Togetherness!' agreed Flint, flinging open the airing cupboard door. 'Oh goody. My lovely egg is still there.'

By now, Darwin was more angry than scared. He didn't know that Dippy had already made the switch. Seeing what he thought was his mother's egg, he felt very protective of it and confronted Flint.

'That's not your egg, it's Mum's!'

'Leave it,' warned Dippy quietly, but Darwin was too cross to let the matter drop. With great courage, he pushed past Mr Cretaceous, jumped up and tried to grab the egg off the shelf, but Flint beat him to it.

'Not so fast,' he sneered, holding the egg out of reach. 'Now then, what shall we do with this egg?'

'Let's have a game of footy with it!' said Mr Cretaceous. 'On me 'ead, boss!'

Flint made as if to throw the egg, then seeing the desperate look on Darwin's face, he decided to tease him further and hung onto it.

'Footy? No. That's not really my game.'

'Phew, thanks, Mr Beastwood. I knew you'd do the right thing in the end,' said Darwin, holding out his hands for the egg.

Flint snatched it away and tucked it under his scaly arm. 'I'm more of a rugby kind of guy!' He grinned, sprinting round the room with the egg wedged in his armpit. 'Come along, Mr C, tackle me!'

The deinosuchus pounded after him, threw himself on the floor and grabbed his boss around the ankles.

'Be careful, it'll break!' wailed Darwin, getting ready to do a dive-catch if Flint fell and dropped the egg.

'Do you hear that? The egg might break!' said

Flint sarcastically. 'You'd better let go of me, Mr Cretaceous. I'd hate to trip. I shouldn't want little Darwin to be an only child.'

'Thank you, Mr Beastwood,' said Darwin. 'Dad said you must have a heart and he was right. Please can I have our egg back now?'

'Of course,' said Flint. 'Come and get it.'

Darwin walked over to him innocently and reached out to take it, but just as he felt the warm shell touch his palm, Flint jerked it away again and started juggling with it.

'Look at me, I'm a jester!' he mocked.

This was too much for Darwin. He leapt up and tried to grab the egg mid-flight, but as Flint tried to dodge him, it flew out of control, bounced off the ceiling and smashed down on

the T. Rex's top hat. As the rotten yolk dripped all over Flint's wedding suit, the room filled with a stinking, suffocating cloud of rotten-egg gas. Darwin's eyes watered. He didn't think he'd ever smelt anything so bad. The carnivores were closest and fell to their knees, choking. Dippy grabbed Darwin by the hand, pulling him towards the fire escape.

'I wish I'd known you'd swapped the eggs when I arrived!' panted Darwin as they raced down the spiral staircase and round to the back of the kitchen. 'Have you got Mum's egg safe?'

'It's under me hat.' Dippy smiled, banging on the kitchen window to get Mrs Stigson's attention and lifting his cap when she turned to look. Seeing the delighted expression on his mother's face, Darwin knew that even needing six baths to wash away the smell of the rotten egg was worth it.

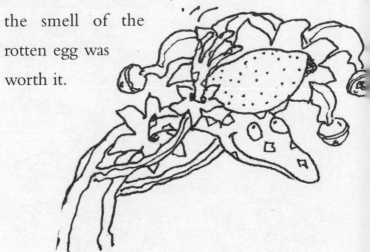

Now that her family had all arrived back at Fossil Street in one piece, a very grateful Mrs Stigson placed her rescued egg back in its rightful nest and put the kettle on.

'Coffee or tea, Phyllis?' she said as the portly mastodon parked herself on the sofa.

'Did you manage to save us any wedding cake?' asked Mrs Merrick. 'Only I'm sure Dippy and Sir Tempest would love a piece.'

'You speak for yourself,' said the triceratops. 'I wouldn't touch it with a bladder on a stick. It'll be full of australopithecus hairs.'

'Fusspot!' she snapped. 'Have you got any ginger snaps, Lydia? I like those.'

Mrs Stigson hunted through her kitchen cupboards, found the biscuits and got out the side plates.

After a short while, Mrs Merrick cocked one of her massive ears. 'Can you hear a cracking noise, Sir Tempest?' she muttered. 'It sounds as if Lydia's cutting the ginger snaps in half. How very mean.'

But Mrs Stigson was doing no such thing.

'Mum, come quickly!' called Darwin. 'The egg's about to hatch!'

Suddenly, all thoughts of biscuits were forgotten as the family and neighbours gathered round the nest, watching and waiting for the new little Stigson to arrive.

'Let's hope it's a stegosaur this time,' joked Mr Stigson.

As the scaly little head broke through the egg, the family likeness was thankfully obvious to everyone.

'She's got her mother's eyes,' said Sir Tempest.

'And her daddy's nose,' cooed Mrs Merrick.

'Let's hope she's got her uncle's brain,' added Loops. 'What are you going to call her, Damian?'

Darwin's little sister looked up at him lovingly. She had a bit of egg stuck to her head like a beret and it was this that made him decide on the name.

'Let's call her Shelly,' he said.

'Smelly?' said Uncle Loops. 'I like it! It's a perfect name for a baby and so easy to remember. Nice one, Dawson!'

'Thanks, Uncle Poops!' said Darwin, laughing.

They'd always had a laugh together, and now he had a sister, it would be *twice* as much fun.

THE UPTOWN AND DOWNTOWN PREHISTORIC SPOTTER'S GUIDE

DINOSAURS

Stegosaurus

(Steg–oh–saw–rus)

Example: The Stigsons

Triceratops

(Try–sair–a–tops)

Example: Sir Tempest

Ankylosaur

(Ank–ee–lo–saw)

Example: Frank and Ernest

Mamenchisaurus

(Mah-men-chee-saw-rus)

Example: Lou Gooby

Tyrannosaurus Rex

(Tie-ran-o-saw-rus Rex)

Example: Flint Beastwood

Velociraptor

(Veh-loss-i-rap-tor)

Example: Liz Vicious

Gallimimus

(Gall-uh-my-mus)

Example: Dippy Egg

OTHER PREHISTORIC CREATURES

Deinosuchus
(Day-no-sook-us)
Example: Mr Cretaceous

Pteranodon
(Tehr-ran-oh-don)
Example:
Terry O'Dactyl

Mastodon
(Mas-toe-don)
Example: Mrs Merrick

Australopithecus
(Oss–tra–lo–pith–ah–cus)
Example: Ozzi

Cynognathus
(Sigh–nog–nay–thus)
Example: Nogs

Darwin, the young stegosaurus, and his family
are throwing a great party, when it is gate-
crashed by T-Rex Flint Beastwood
and his scary gang.

Will war break out between the dinosaurs or
can Boris, the Mayor, bring peace with the
brilliant idea of . . . the Olympic Games?

DINOSAURS IN DISGUISE

T. Rex Flint Beastwood is furious! Dippy has
gone missing in the forest, just when Flint
needed him to clean his toenails!

When Darwin the stegosaurus goes missing
too, the herbivores send out a search party. But
it's dangerous in the woods, with Flint's deadly
carnivore gang AND a scary new dinosaur! So
they come up with a brilliant idea – to disguise
themselves as trees . . .